Ghostly Tales of Wisconsin

Dedication:

For my friends Chris and Amy, who dare to live in "the most haunted state in America."

A special thank you to everyone who willingly shared their ghost stories and who allowed me to put their tales into this collection. I appreciate your time and patience. I would also like to thank the many people who gave me guidance and pointed me in the right direction during the process of researching this book.

In some instances, names and locations have been changed at the request of sources.

Content Warning: This book contains several references to suicide and may not be appropriate for all audiences.

Cover design by Travis Bryant and Scott McGrew
Text design by Karla Linder
Edited by Emily Beaumont

All images copyrighted.
Images used under license from Shutterstock.com:
Covers and silhouettes: **Alexander_P:** spiderweb;
Arthur Balitskii: spider; **Elena Pimonova:** tree
Interior: **Fer Gregory:** 75; **katalinks:** 49; **Vladimir Mulder:** 97; **Melinda Nagy:** 29; **Arend Trent:** 1

10 9 8 7 6 5 4 3 2 1
Ghostly Tales of Wisconsin
First Edition 2009
Second Edition 2022
Copyright © 2009 and 2022 by Ryan Jacobson
Published by Adventure Publications
310 Garfield Street South
Cambridge, Minnesota 55008
(800) 678-7006
www.adventurepublications.net
All rights reserved
Printed in the U.S.A.
ISBN 978-1-64755-311-1 (pbk.); eISBN 978-1-64755-312-8

Ghostly Tales of Wisconsin

Ryan Jacobson

Table of Contents

HAUNTED HOTELS

SEVEN CEMETERIES

Preface

This chilling collection was put together through countless hours of research, interviews, and fact-checking. It includes many of Wisconsin's most famous haunts, some of the state's more obscure ghost stories, and even a few terrifying tales that have never before been recorded.

The narratives were written using the information gathered, but some of the details were provided to me as checklists of unexplainable occurrences rather than *Ghostly Tales*. Therefore, while the information remains accurate, some of the scenarios (and characters) were reinterpreted for dramatic effect.

I can neither verify the validity of each claim nor the existence of supernatural beings, but I can assure you that the portrayals of the spirits in this book are as accurate as possible.

Enjoy!

Haunted Homes

Summerwind Scares

An Uninvited Guest

The property was glorious to behold. Sitting along the crystal-blue waters of West Bay Lake in northeastern Wisconsin—just a stone's throw from Canada—the fishing lodge was a hideaway from the rest of the world, tucked within a plush, green forest.

"It's perfect," Robert Lamont proclaimed, inhaling a deep breath of clean Wisconsin air. "We'll turn it into our family's summer getaway."

Thus it was decided: The man who would later become President Herbert Hoover's Secretary of Commerce bought the land in 1916. He hired contractors to turn the wooden lodge into Summerwind, a mansion that history would remember as the Badger State's most haunted home.

For 20 years, the gentleman and his wife enjoyed the house without incident. However, they often grew tired of the superstitious housekeepers' warnings. "I'm telling you, Mr. Lamont," said one of the servants, "we've seen shadows. We've heard voices. This place is haunted."

"And I'm telling you," the homeowner answered sternly, "any more talk of ghosts, and I may become one myself."

Lamont sat down with his wife in their country-style kitchen and enjoyed a delicious lunch, followed by a tasty dessert. But to the Lamonts' astonishment, their meal was soon interrupted by a sudden, violent shaking.

"The basement door," cried Mrs. Lamont. "What on earth is happening?"

"I don't know," admitted her husband, as he stared at the vibrating entrance. He stood and reached into a nearby drawer where his pistol was kept.

Thud!

The basement door flew open, banging against the wall. A tall, dark-haired man stepped into the room. His face was unfamiliar to Lamont, but the scowl he wore suggested that he was out for blood.

The door slammed closed behind the stranger as he stepped toward Lamont's wife.

Not waiting to learn of the intruder's intent, Lamont grabbed his gun, aimed it at the man's chest and fired two shots. Both bullets passed harmlessly through the visitor, lodging into the basement door.

"My word," the homeowner exclaimed. "He's not human. He's a ghost!"

An instant later, the specter was gone. The terrified couple performed their own disappearing act, fleeing the mansion immediately.

Hinshaw Horrors

By the early 1970s, Summerwind had become something of a fixer-upper. The paint was faded and chipped. Several windows were shattered. Nearly every interior room required renovating. Nevertheless, Ginger and Arnold Hinshaw were not deterred.

"I love it, Arnold," Ginger said. "I just love it."

Her husband nodded. "It needs a little work, but there's so much potential. This could be the house of our dreams."

The couple purchased the old mansion and moved their family, including four children, inside.

Almost immediately, even the most mundane tasks became frightful adventures. The kids feared walking the hallways, as eerie shadows danced about. Arnold and Ginger could rarely move from one room to the next without hearing the chilling whispers of an unseen presence. Even turning on the water was a venture into the unknown, as appliances such as the water pump and hot water heater sometimes failed inexplicably. Yet, the machines always managed to fix themselves a short while later.

And then, on one occasion, the ghost almost took Arnold's life.

"See you later," the man yelled upstairs to his spouse, who was awake and already preparing the home for its first round of renovations.

"Have a good day at work," she hollered back.

Arnold smiled as he stepped outside, into the brisk morning air. He marched across the lawn toward his car.

WHOOSH!

The vehicle was suddenly ablaze.

Arnold leapt back, nearly catching on fire himself. He frantically dashed around the yard, checking first to ensure that none of the children were nearby and second to see if anyone else—an arsonist, perhaps—was present.

He found no one.

Retreating safely away from the blaze, Arnold could do nothing else—except watch helplessly as flames engulfed his automobile.

To make matters worse, the Hinshaws began having problems with the construction workers they had hired.

"What do you mean you can't work here anymore?" Arnold demanded.

"I mean the crew won't go inside," said the foreman. "They've been telling all sorts of tales, but the bottom line is this: Your place gives them—us—the creeps. You'll have to find another team to take over."

Unfortunately for the Hinshaws, replacement laborers proved just as difficult to secure, leaving the family to do the work themselves.

"Ginger, have you seen this shoe drawer?" Arnold asked his wife, as he scoured the bedroom closet.

"The one built into the wall?" she answered, applying a fresh coat of color to a nearby surface. "Yes, I have. Can you take it out? I want to paint it."

Arnold did as Ginger requested and, to his surprise, discovered a dark crawl space hidden behind the closet.

"What's this?" said Arnold, grabbing a flashlight. "What's what?" responded his wife, but she was too late to catch her husband, who had already wedged himself halfway into the opening.

The man slowly panned his light around the area, unsure of what he might find back there. However, he never expected to discover . . .

"Yah!" he yelped, scurrying out in a panic. "What is it?" asked Ginger.

"A dead animal. A bear or something."

"How in heaven would a bear get in there?"

"It probably crawled inside while the house was being built and got stuck," said Arnold. "Let me get a closer look."

He tried to squeeze farther into the hidden space, but he was too big. So when the children returned from school, his daughter Mary bravely volunteered.

"Take the flashlight," said her father. "Crawl inside and tell us what you see."

Mary disappeared into the mysterious opening, as the rest of the family anxiously waited for her report. However, what followed was a terrified, bloodcurdling scream.

"It's a person, Dad! It's a person!"

The carcass that Arnold had glimpsed was, in truth, an arm, part of a leg, and the black-haired skull of a human.

The Hinshaws chose not to disclose the gruesome find to police officials. (Later, when the story was reported, the explanation given was that the family believed the body was too old. They thought any crime committed would have occurred so long ago that police would not be able to do anything about it.) Arnold and Ginger left the corpse alone, abandoning it where they had found it, once again entombing it behind the drawer.

As the story goes, this was when the Hinshaw family began to unravel—and when Arnold became obsessed with playing the Hammond organ he and his wife had purchased.

The organ's frantic, nonsensical song echoed through the mansion. Each macabre note sent a chill down Ginger's spine. Huddled beside her, the children wept.

She glanced at the clock. It was after 2 in the morning. Ginger composed herself, took a deep breath and once again trekked downstairs, where Arnold pounded the organ keys, sweat dripping from his face.

"Arnold," said Ginger. "You're scaring the children." He ignored her.

"Arnold, please stop."

Once again, her husband did not respond.

"Are you listening?" she snapped, grabbing his arm.

He spun toward his wife, his eyes blazing wildly. "I can't stop. I can't ever stop. The demons make me play!" He kept slamming his hands against the organ, time and again, louder and faster than before.

Ginger trudged back up the stairs, crying. When she reached the bedroom where the children were hiding, she once again stepped inside, this time locking the door behind her.

Within weeks, Arnold suffered a nervous breakdown, and Ginger reportedly attempted to kill herself. Arnold was hospitalized, leaving his wife to care for the children. She put Summerwind behind her and moved to Granton to live with her parents.

Ginger and Arnold eventually divorced, and the woman slowly recovered from her Summerwind ordeal. She once again found stability, marrying a man named George Olsen. At last, she'd put the ghosts of Summerwind to bed forever—or so she thought.

But then, a few years later, Ginger's father informed his daughter that he intended to buy Summerwind.

The Carver Effect

"The location alone will make it a gold mine," said Ginger's dad, Raymond Bober. "If we turn the old mansion into a restaurant and an inn, we'll attract a ton of paying customers. We'll make a fortune!"

A popcorn vendor and an entrepreneur, Raymond had his heart set on purchasing the property. Along with his wife, Marie, and his son, Karl, he dreamed of transforming Summerwind into a lucrative business.

"You don't understand," pleaded his daughter. "I can't tell you why, but there's something about the place. It's a disaster waiting to happen. Please, don't buy it. Please!"

Raymond smiled warmly at his frightened daughter. "I already know what you don't want to tell me, Ginger. Summerwind is haunted." He patted her arm gently. "But I can also tell you something else. I know who the ghost is."

Ginger stared at her father in disbelief. "How could you? How is that possible?"

"I've been in contact with the spirit through dreams and trances—and even a Ouija board. It's the ghost of Jonathan Carver, an eighteenth-century British explorer."

Ginger shook her head. "Even if that's true, it won't help you. Summerwind tore our lives apart!"

"Carver's ghost just wants a little help. That's all. The Sioux Indians gave him a deed granting him the rights to the northern third of Wisconsin. It's in a sealed box inside Summerwind's foundation. If we find it, Carver will leave us alone."

Ginger found little comfort in her father's revelation, but she could not prevent him from purchasing the mansion. She begrudgingly agreed to visit the home with Raymond, Karl, and her new husband, George.

The four of them spent several hours checking over the place, and before long they entered the bedroom that housed the hidden tomb. Ginger held her breath as George entered the closet, until at last she couldn't take it anymore.

"No, no, no! Get out of there. Get away!" She begged everyone to leave, almost to the point of hysteria.

Ginger's family rushed her downstairs and into the kitchen, giving her an opportunity to calm herself.

She swallowed hard, took a deep breath and at last said, "There's something I need to tell you." With that, she shared all of the details about the body concealed within the closet.

Her warning didn't stop Raymond. Instead, it seemed to pique his interest. Karl volunteered to venture into the closet (as Raymond and George were too large to fit). On all fours, staring at the crawl space, he stuck his hand toward his father. "Give me the flashlight."

Karl carefully slipped inside, while Ginger and the others waited in dreadful anticipation. They expected him to re-emerge at any moment, perhaps holding a skull in one hand. Instead, after a painfully long moment of silence, Karl finally shouted, "There's nothing in here!"

The corpse was gone.

Over Labor Day weekend, Karl visited the mansion to get an estimate on some work that needed completing. While he was alone there, a thunderstorm had him darting through the upstairs hallway, closing the open windows.

"Karl," said a distinct, haunting voice.

The young man stopped, his heart racing—not from the exertion but from the frightful sound he had heard.

"Karl," the voice called once again.

Cautiously, Ginger's brother searched the hallway. No one else was present.

Certain that he was alone but also knowing his name had been called, Karl finished closing the windows and returned downstairs. But as he entered the front room, he heard an unmistakable echo.

Bang!

Bang!

A gun had been fired in the kitchen—twice.

Karl hurried to investigate, finding the room thick with smoke and smelling of gunpowder. But once again, his search of the premises turned up no one. In fact, all of the doors were locked.

It was then that Karl noticed the bullets left behind by Robert Lamont so many years ago. And that was enough to convince him to pack up and leave, which he did that very afternoon.

From there, the Bobers' problems only grew worse. Similar to the difficulties that Ginger and her first husband had faced, Raymond found it nearly impossible to keep construction workers on the job.

"Every time we measure this room," said one laborer, "it's a different size."

"How is that possible?" Bober asked.

"I don't know, but the number never matches the blueprints. And if we can't measure it, we can't fix it."

Furthermore, photographs taken at different times also seemed to indicate that the house had grown. In one instance, a picture Raymond snapped of the living room revealed a startling detail.

"Look at the windows," said Ginger, holding up the photograph. "It shows the very curtains I brought home with me when we moved out!"

Sure enough, all of the windows were curtained in the picture, but there were no curtains in the room.

Given all of these strange happenings, it's no wonder why Raymond and his family members spent their nights at Summerwind in an RV, rather than sleeping inside the house. And, not surprisingly, Raymond eventually had to abandon his dreams of turning the haunted mansion into a restaurant and inn. However, he did log several days in Summerwind's basement, searching for Jonathan Carver's deed and even chipping away at the foundation, but the document was never found.

Raymond later wrote a book about his supernatural communications with the ghost of Jonathan Carver. *The Carver Effect* was published in 1979.

The Fate of Summerwind

By the early 1980s, the old house sat abandoned and empty. It fell into ruin—windows broken, wood rotting, doors missing—but the mansion's feeble condition did not deter three investors from purchasing the place in 1986.

Plans for the site were once again thwarted, this time by Mother Nature. Lightning struck Summerwind during a ferocious thunderstorm in June of 1988, burning the entire structure to the ground and leaving only the foundation, stone steps, and a chimney behind.

Neighborhood Nightmare

The neighborhood was different. Darker. Everyone could sense it, but no one wanted to talk about it. Who could blame them, though? Suicide wasn't exactly the most welcome of subject matters. The topic of ghosts was even more taboo.

The trouble had begun in La Crosse on August 1, 1904, the day that Nicolai Holmbo hanged himself in the front room of his house. From the moment his body was found, the neighborhood was shaken to its core. After all, those sorts of tragedies weren't supposed to happen so close to home. But as Holmbo's neighbors soon discovered, suicide was only the first of many horrors to come.

A husband and wife enjoying a quiet evening stroll were among the first to encounter Holmbo's ghost.

"Oh, Henry, look at that!" exclaimed Mrs. Carlson, as the couple happened past the vacant house.

A startled Mr. Carlson flinched at the frantic tone in his wife's voice. But when he saw what had frightened her in the first place, his blood ran cold.

A white-shrouded phantom stood at one of the house's windows. The ghostly specter remained motionless for a moment, but then it became animated, swinging its arms and gesturing wildly.

Mr. and Mrs. Carlson hurried away from the ghastly site. They chose not to walk past that house again.

Furthermore, a neighbor living across the street was taken aback by the brilliant lights that shone from within the home almost every night.

"It's not natural," he told his wife. "There's something evil inside that house."

As if to confirm his suspicions, terrible, disheartening cries began to emanate from within the Holmbo residence. "That does it," declared the neighbor. "I'm going to fetch the police."

When officers arrived on the scene, the screams grew louder. The policemen rushed toward the empty house. However, the instant they stepped foot onto the yard, the lights went out and the cries stopped.

A thorough search of the place turned up empty. No one was found inside.

Not surprisingly, the old Holmbo residence remained vacant for several decades. However, in recent years, it has once again become a private residence.

Night Frights

Karen Anderson had a choice to make. She'd earned enough high school credits to graduate a semester early. So now she could either stay home and bring in a little extra income, or she could move to Wausau to live with her father.

It wasn't a difficult decision.

"You guys got divorced a long time ago," Karen told her mother. "And that was right for you. But this is a chance for me to get to know my dad. I don't think I can pass it up."

Thus, craving an opportunity to bond with a man who was little more than a stranger, Karen moved to the central Wisconsin city in 1982, leaving her mom and her younger sister, Sheryl, behind.

Almost immediately, Karen had second thoughts. Upon entering her father's house, she felt uneasy, uncomfortable. But she wasn't certain whether it was the home itself or her father's new wife, Stephanie, that caused the eerie sensation.

This wasn't the stereotypical stepmother-stepdaughter resentment, though. As Karen told her sister in a telephone conversation, "She's into all sorts of weird stuff. I think she's a witch, Sheryl."

True enough, the woman openly dabbled in the occult and in dark magic. Conversely, Stephanie was obsessed with religion and with the Bible. She fanatically read the Good Book, maintaining stacks of scribbled notes and messages about it.

Stephanie's cats also acted in a bizarre fashion. Whenever Karen stood to leave a room, the felines darted out before her, ran directly to the place she was headed and waited, staring at her with their piercing eyes. It was as if the cats somehow knew where Karen was going—as if they could read her mind.

The teenaged girl was overwhelmed with relief when, three weeks into her stay, Sheryl came to visit. The sisters chose to share a double bed in the extra bedroom.

"Is it just me, or do you get a bad vibe in here?" Sheryl asked, as she unpacked her suitcase.

Karen gestured toward the alcove beyond Sheryl's side of the bed. "There's a cold spot over there. It's the only place inside the entire house where Stephanie's dogs ever go to the bathroom."

Sheryl frowned. "What does that mean?"

"It means I like to stay on this side of the room."

Later that night, at just before midnight, Karen was shaken awake by her younger sister.

"What's wrong?" Karen asked, her voice groggy.

"I can't sleep," whispered Sheryl. "I keep thinking there's something behind me in that alcove."

"It's just your imagination. Now try to get some rest."

"If it's just my imagination, can we switch sides?"

Karen thought for a moment and then decided, "No."

She rolled onto her side, away from her sister, signaling the end of the conversation.

A few hours later, Karen was awakened again. However, this time, it wasn't her sister that stirred her. She bolted upright in bed, surprised to see Sheryl doing the same.

"What happened?" asked Karen.

"I don't know," said Sheryl. "I just woke up."

"Me too, but why? Did you hear anything?"

"No, it was more like a feeling. A really bad feeling."

Karen understood exactly what her sister meant. The room seemed clouded by a thick sense of foreboding.

Sleep did not come easily after that.

Unfortunately, the daylight hours brought little comfort for the teens. Sheryl confessed to her older sister that the adults—their father and their stepmother—did not seem to be on their side.

Karen felt the same way.

Each girl was the other's only ally in the house. They could not discuss their fears with their parents, and the nightly task of sleeping in that room was an even more frightful ordeal.

Three nights later, Karen was again awakened. And again, she sat upright in bed at the same instant Sheryl did. However, this time, the reason was apparent.

As Karen stared into the alcove, horrified, she heard an audible gasp from her sister, followed by a soft whimper. Karen wanted to scream, but she could not find her voice. Instead, she stared silently at the ghastly specter of a man hanging from the ceiling by his necktie!

Almost a week later, Karen received a phone call from Sheryl, who was safely back home with her mother.

"Karen, I need to tell you about the dream I had last night," Sheryl whispered, almost afraid to speak the words aloud. "I was in that bedroom again, and I walked over to the alcove. I pulled up the carpeting on the floor, and I found a puddle of dried blood."

Karen paused, and then she said, "It was just a dream," although it was more for her own sake than for her sister's.

"Are you going to check? " Sheryl asked. "Under the carpet, I mean."

"No. I'm never going in that room again."

Years later, Karen's father and Stephanie divorced. The house still belongs to Stephanie's family, but neither Karen nor Sheryl has visited it in more than 20 years.

Something Scary
on TV

The Evenson family's first television was a black-and-white machine, and it was small— its screen a mere 13 inches. However, it must have weighed 70 pounds. It picked up exactly three channels, although the reception wasn't great on any of them. Furthermore, there was no remote control for this ancient electronic device. In order to activate it, one had to stand, walk over to it, and pull the knob.

The family's oldest son, Scott, loved that television. For him, Friday night was the best part of every week. That was when his family gathered inside the living room of their small home near Madison, ate pizza, and watched whichever channel came in the clearest.

The following years brought new technologies. Soon Scott's family had a color console TV, and the black-and-white box was moved into the kitchen. Then, in 1983, when Scott was 12 years old, the television was relegated to the upstairs bedroom he shared with his brother, Max.

Most children Scott's age would have been thrilled with a TV, and at first Scott was no different. However, all of that changed just a few days after the machine was moved to the second floor. That's when the haunting began.

It was a typically steamy July night, so Scott had been granted permission to leave a fan running in the bedroom window. It didn't help; he fell asleep sweating. But strangely, when Scott awoke at 1 a.m., he was chilled to the bone.

The boy crawled out of bed and scurried toward the fan in order to shut it off. But he only made it halfway to the window.

Click!

Scott heard the TV's knob being pulled. He swung around to scold his brother, but Max was still in bed—asleep. Scott could only watch in terror as the screen came to life, illuminating the room. The TV was on, but no one had touched the controls!

The screen's black-and-white static reminded Scott of *Poltergeist*, one of his family's favorite horror films. The mental connection served only to heighten his fright.

Forgetting his younger brother, Scott darted into the hall and down the stairs. He burst into his parents' room and dove onto their bed. "Mom, Dad, wake up!"

"What is it, honey?" his mother asked sleepily, as she rolled onto her side.

Scott tried to speak, but all he could do was mutter, "Upstairs . . . ghost."

The boy's parents calmed Scott and waited as he explained what had happened. They led him back to his room, where the fan was still running but the TV was off (and Max was sound asleep).

"See? It was just a bad dream," his mother whispered. "Everything is as normal as can be."

His father walked over to the fan and unplugged it. "There you go, buddy. Now hop into bed. You'll be asleep in a snap."

By the time his parents left the bedroom, Scott was convinced that nothing extraordinary had happened. And if that had been the end of the tale, he probably would have lived the remainder of his life believing it. However . . .

Click!
The TV was on again.

It was the fourth night this week that the knob had been pulled by an invisible force. But this time was no less scary than the first.

Scott and Max screamed. Then, once again, they raced to their parents' bed.

Mom and Dad were not pleased to see them.

"That's it!" exclaimed Mr. Evenson. "I've had enough of this ghost business. Tomorrow, I'm taking that TV to the secondhand store."

True to his word, Scott's father removed the television from the house early the next morning. And with the machine gone, the Evenson brothers' ghostly encounters came to an abrupt end.

The Woman in White

Anna Hurley knew the history of her family's house. The 15-year-old girl had watched it being built on an old hay field outside the central Wisconsin town of Stratford. So why, then, did she see what she had seen?

It was the spring of 2000, and her brothers were gone to college. The house was empty except for her mother and herself, but one of the vacant bedrooms troubled the girl. Located at the base of an open stairway, the room often drew the attention of Anna's dog. The tiny pooch could be seen sitting before the door, barking into the room. Plus, the walls made strange noises, as if they were bending.

Anna could not walk past the mysterious bedroom without getting a paranoid feeling, so she made a habit of keeping the door to the room closed.

It did little good. Every day, when she returned home from school, Anna would find the door open again.

After one particularly grueling day of learning, the teenager took a nap on the living room couch.

Thump!

The noise awakened Anna. She lifted her head. "Mom?"

The girl's mother was not the source of the sound. Instead, Anna's eyes widened as she spied the figure of a young woman in a flowing, white, misty dress. She was hovering before the bedroom door!

The specter turned and looked at the girl, and then suddenly disappeared. As Anna later described the moment, it was as if the spirit had been sucked into the bedroom.

Petrified, Anna refused to believe what she had seen. She chose not to tell a soul.

Within months, for unrelated reasons, Anna's mother decided to move the two of them into town. However, as they packed and made preparations to sell the house, the teenaged girl's unease grew. She sensed that the ghost was irritated, even annoyed, that they were leaving.

Nothing came of those feelings, though, until Anna's final night in that house. It was October, and the place was empty. Anna had been granted permission to have two friends spend the night, camping in sleeping bags on the living room floor.

As far as Anna knew, the night was otherwise unremarkable. But the next morning, one of her friends told quite a tale.

"Anna, something weird happened last night."

The girl gave her friend a puzzled look. "Really? What do you mean?"

"I don't know how to say this without sounding crazy," the friend explained. "But, well, never mind."

"Tell me," pleaded Anna, suspecting that she knew what her friend was unwilling to share.

"Well, something woke me up last night. A noise. And I think I saw a ghost: a woman dressed in white."

Anna's friend also went on to say that the specter had walked upstairs and disappeared in a fashion similar to what Anna witnessed seven months earlier.

The identical report was enough to convince Anna that she had seen an apparition. So at last she revealed her own experience to her two friends.

In the years since the Hurleys moved out, no ghostly encounters have been reported. But for Anna, the spirit that visited her old house opened the girl's mind to a belief in the paranormal.

School
Spirits

The Sickly Specter

Being married to the president of Saint John's Military Academy certainly has its privileges, thought Mrs. Sidney Thomas Smythe as she strolled down a long corridor on her way to the large entrance hall. *After all, look at this glorious house.*

She was referring to the mansion in which she lived, Rosslynne Manse. Built by her husband on the academy grounds near the town of Delafield, the place had been modeled after the Scottish home of Dr. Smythe's uncle. Thus, it was given a Scottish name. The incomparable structure was distinguished by its towering stone fireplace and its spacious porches.

The year was 1905. Mrs. Smythe was alone in the house—or so she thought. Daydreaming about her beloved Rosslynne Manse, she stepped into the vast entrance hall and saw a frightful sight: Sitting in a rocking chair beside a large window was a pale—albeit well-dressed—man.

Fearing that an intruder had broken into her home, Mrs. Smythe let out a startled scream and called for help. But suddenly, the sickly man disappeared before her eyes!

Later she told her husband, "It must have been a ghost, but he appeared to be in the final stages of some horrible, fatal disease."

Never one to doubt his wife's judgment, Dr. Smythe nodded. "Rosslynne Manse wasn't the first home built on this property. We'll find an explanation about this strange phenomenon."

Their quest for knowledge led them to interview one of the property's old gardeners.

"The Ashby family used to live here," said the gardener. "They had a son-in-law who died of tuberculosis. He was a fine young gentleman and a snappy dresser. But by the end, when the disease took him, he looked pretty bad off."

Mrs. Smythe gasped. "That's exactly who I saw!"

More than a decade later, the Smythes' 20-year-old son, Charles, had his own run-in with the apparition. It was in the same room, in nearly the same place. This time, the ghost was standing, his hands clasped behind his back. The family dog, who had been walking beside Charles, cowered in terror. But within moments, the spirit had vanished.

Rosslynne Manse burned to the ground in a 1981 fire-training exercise, and the land has since become open grounds for the military academy. However, some believe that, while the building is gone, the spirit remains.

A Spirit Scorned

Katelyn Moe was as excited as any freshman, living away from her Eau Claire family for the first time in her life.

"I can't believe I'm here," she whispered to herself as she wandered the grounds of Northland College.

Renowned for its environmental liberal arts program, the school had a small-town appeal to it. Plus, its setting, as much as anything else, had drawn Katelyn there. Located in Ashland, in northwestern Wisconsin, the college was within view of Lake Superior. Its dormitories, halls, and other buildings were spread out among winding trails and stands of trees that provided a unique North Woods flair. Strolling past Dexter Library, Katelyn encountered a familiar face: Sarah Dehan, an old softball teammate who was two years her senior.

"Where are you living?" Sarah asked, following a few minutes of small talk.

"Over in Memorial Hall," said Katelyn.

"Whoa," whistled Sarah. "Have you heard any of the ghost stories?"

Katelyn's mouth dropped open. "No, and I don't really think I want to."

Sarah laughed. "They're just stories. Apparently, some girl killed herself a while back by jumping down the elevator shaft. Now she haunts the building."

"Yeah, right," said Katelyn sarcastically, although she already wished her former teammate hadn't told her.

Sarah wasn't finished. "Don't bring any guys inside either," the college junior warned. "The ghost doesn't like them. In fact, some people think she didn't even kill herself. They think her old boyfriend pushed her."

Having already heard too much, Katelyn ended the conversation as politely as she could, and then she hurried away. She entered her three-story dormitory, desperately trying to control her overactive imagination.

Later that night, Katelyn was awakened by the chime of her computer starting up. She shot out of bed and turned on the lights, but no one else was there. The computer had turned on all by itself!

In case that wasn't enough, the printer also roared to life, duplicating a text document Katelyn had saved onto her desktop.

Much to the dismay of Katelyn (and to her roommate, who arrived a couple of days later), the ghostly incidents began happening on a regular basis. In fact, they occurred so often that Katelyn kept her computer and her printer unplugged whenever she wasn't using them.

It was a simple solution to the problem, but there was little Katelyn could do when mysterious handprints began appearing in her room.

Thoroughly frightened and unable to switch residence halls, Katelyn did the only thing she could, heeding Sarah's sage advice not to bring any young men into the building. Eventually, the appearance of handprints subsided.

The second half of the year brought only a few unexplainable occurrences, and Katelyn grew accustomed to the ghostly presence. She later moved into a different hall, following her first year at Northland College, and while others may scoff at the rumored spirit that haunts Memorial Hall, Katelyn remains a firm believer.

Gangster Ghost

Robyn Klink didn't like walking her younger brother to school. The area around Huntley Elementary in Appleton gave her the creeps. In fact, while she was there, she often felt as if she were being watched or followed. She had to wonder if her fourth-grade sibling picked up on the eerie sensation, as well, or if he were simply too young to care.

Part of the problem was that the 14-year-old girl knew the stories about the neighborhood's gangster ghost, and perhaps that contributed to her fears. "Marky," as the specter was called, had worked for the mob in the late 1920s (while he was still alive), and he was rumored to be a distant relative of the old crime boss, Lucky Luciano.

The girl could not remember how Marky died or why he had chosen to haunt this particular neighborhood, but she knew a lot of people—including herself—who believed his spirit was still around.

Her best friend, Becky, had told Robyn that she'd seen Marky from her bedroom window one night. "He was in the street," Becky had said, "bragging about himself to some older kids walking by. I knew it was him because he was wearing these weird, old-fashioned clothes."

Robyn dropped off her brother at the school playground, where dozens of children ran and danced about. Then she began on her way to meet Becky, whose mother would drive them both to their middle school.

Turning from Byrd Street onto Owaissa Street, every muscle in Robyn's body tensed. On the sidewalk ahead of her, marching in her direction, was a teenaged boy who couldn't have been more than three or four years older than she. Much to Robyn's horror, the boy was wearing an outfit straight from the 1920s!

She spun on her heels and began walking—more quickly—in the other direction, away from Becky's house and away from the older teen.

"Hey," yelled the boy. "Hold it right there."

Robyn heard him start to run and glanced backward. He was nearly to her. Too late, she began to sprint as well, but she felt Marky grip her arm and squeeze tightly.

He yanked her hard and spun her toward him. "What's your problem?" the spirit demanded.

Robyn's jacket buttons snapped open, revealing her purple shirt underneath. The girl watched, bewildered, as Marky caught a glimpse of the shirt, his eyes widening in a panicked rage.

The specter began to jump up and down, clutching his head like a madman. "No," he screamed. "It's purple! I hate purple!"

Robyn didn't understand why, but she was glad that he did.

As if to dispel any doubt that he was the ghost of a long-deceased mobster, Marky vanished before her eyes.

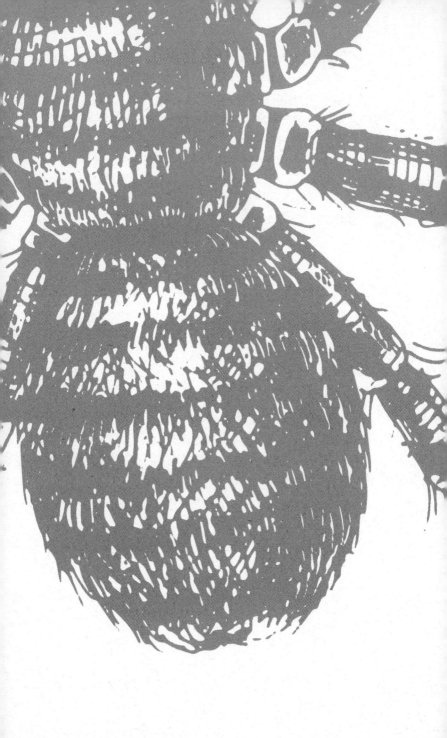

"Holy" Ghost

It was the last place she wanted to be. Sister Augusta (as she came to be called) was having a hard enough time at her Episcopal girls' school in Chicago. But to be sent here, to a retreat at Kemper Hall in Kenosha, Wisconsin, to be subjected to the stern rule of Mother Superior Margaret Clare, the nun who ran the place, this was more than Sister Augusta could bear.

Physically and emotionally exhausted from months of hard work, she requested time off, a request that was reportedly granted. Nevertheless, distraught because she'd been forced to attend an all-girls school, leaving the love of her life behind, Sister Augusta took matters into her own hands. On January 2, 1900, the young woman mysteriously disappeared from the mansion named after Wisconsin's first Episcopal bishop, Jackson Kemper, leaving all of her belongings behind.

Telegrams were sent to relatives in Chicago and Saint Louis, but no trace of Sister Augusta could be found. However, on January 5, a notice was released from Kemper Hall, informing newspapers that the young woman had been located in Springfield, Missouri.

The statement turned out to be untrue.

On the afternoon of January 8, a child named Bertha Smith and her younger brother were playing near the Lake Michigan beach off Seminary Street (now 65th Street). They spied a black-robed body floating in the water and hurried home to tell their mother. Not long thereafter, the police pulled the corpse of Sister Augusta from the lake. She had apparently taken her own life.

Stairwell Specter

The tired, old bakery worker wandered down the long corridor. She had heard the tragic, 30-year-old saga of Sister Augusta, but it was the farthest thing from her mind. At least, it was until she opened the stairwell door.

She stepped through the entrance, turning to walk up the stairs, when she gasped. "Holy Mary, Mother of God!"

Floating above her—seemingly in slow motion—was the deceased young woman's ghost.

The bakery worker hurried into the kitchen. "Everyone! Everyone! Come quickly!"

She rushed her fellow employees to the stairwell, but by the time they arrived, the specter had vanished.

Gymnasium Ghost

Being alone in old buildings didn't usually give Betty the creeps. But as the 1985 Lakeside Players theater group actress stood in Kemper Hall's gymnasium (now

Simmons Auditorium), the hair on the back of her neck stood up. She felt goosebumps rising on her flesh.

There's something off about this place, thought Betty.

Out of the corner of her eye, she caught a glimpse of what appeared to be the figure of a young woman (Sister Augusta), and she spun toward the back wall.

Thud, thud, thud, thud.

Footsteps. They were rushing up the balcony steps.

Betty curiously checked the staircase—and the entire gym—but no trace of anyone else was found.

The Sobbing Spirit

Lori Hartman jumped back with a start as the young nun frantically sped past her.

"Whoa, she's in a hurry," Lori said to her husband, Jerry, watching as the nun disappeared around a distant corner. "What do you suppose that was about?"

"Who knows?" her husband shrugged. Then he added, jokingly, "It's not every day that you see a nun running for her life, though."

As they neared the spot where the nun had turned, they were struck to hear the soft sound of crying. Lori and Jerry glanced at each other, quizzically, as they continued onward toward the noise.

"That poor, poor woman," whispered Lori, trying to be discreet. "I wonder what's wrong?"

She stepped around the corner, expecting to find the nun huddled in some dark corner, weeping. However, the instant that Lori did so, the crying ceased. No one else was there. The nun, just like the heartbreaking sound of sobbing, was gone.

A Frightful Feature

The local news station had a great idea for their 1997 Halloween-related feature: They'd film a segment within the haunted, old girls' school, hoping to capture evidence of Sister Augusta's ghost. Unfortunately, the crew who went inside was disappointed. Nothing extraordinary happened during their stay—or so they thought.

The man who edited the tape found that every time a portrait of the campus's founder, Charles Durkee, was filmed, the footage mysteriously became distorted with static. But as soon as the camera panned away, the screen returned to normal. The bizarre anomaly happened whenever the portrait was filmed, and its occurrence could never be explained.

The Hanging Janitor

Bobby Goneau burst out of the old, abandoned grade school at a sprint.

He looks like he's seen a ghost, thought his best friend, Joey Leonard. *Maybe he has.*

The two teens had gathered outside the condemned school in Argonne with nearly a dozen of their friends and classmates. Rumor had it that the place was haunted, and each of them planned to go inside alone to find out. Bobby had volunteered to go first, and from the look on his face as he rejoined the others, he had definitely seen something.

"What happened?" Joey asked his deathly pale friend. Bobby didn't reply. He simply shook his head in disbelief. "You're next," one of the oldest boys in the group decided, gesturing toward Joey.

The boy glanced once more at the fearful expression on Bobby's face and then toward the teetering old school, which looked as if a strong wind might topple it. He took a deep breath, steeled his nerves, and began to walk.

As he entered the school's second-floor storage area (which reminded him a little of his grandparents' neglected garage), Joey thought of the rumor that had brought his friend group here in the first place. Apparently, a janitor had committed suicide in the 1950s, hanging himself in the very room where Joey now stood.

The teenager sensed himself beginning to panic, and the fact that the room was almost pitch black served only to heighten Joey's fears. Nevertheless, he was going to do what he had come to do.

With a flashlight in hand, Joey cautiously stepped through the filthy, spidery room and to the far wall. The dozens of names scrawled onto it reminded Joey that he was not the first to attempt this dare.

"Here goes nothing," he said, reaching into his pocket and pulling out a black permanent marker.

His hands trembled slightly, as he meticulously drew each letter of his name alongside those of so many other brave teens who'd already met this challenge.

Then, when he finished writing, he waited.

A minute seemed like an eternity, and Joey didn't plan on standing there any longer.

Did I really expect something supernatural to happen? he asked himself, as he started toward the door, the quickness of his pace revealing his nervousness.

Joey heard the ghost before he saw it. The bloodcurdling moan stopped him in his tracks. It had come from almost directly above him.

Slowly, with his hands shaking so badly that he almost couldn't hold the flashlight, he raised the beam skyward.

Above him, hanging from the rafters, was a terrifying vision of the janitor.

Like his best friend before him, Joey erupted from the school at a run. He was the last of his group to enter the cursed room.

Nowadays, the Old Argonne Grade School is no more. A few years after the building was condemned in the early 1990s—and less than a year following Joey's frightful encounter—it was destroyed. All that remains is a gravel driveway that leads to an empty lot.

Murders
and **Mysteries**

Gein's Ghosts

"Care to guess how many people Ed Gein is known to have killed?" John Stratman asked, as his car approached the town of Plainfield.

"Um, 15," said his girlfriend, Sarah Petersen. Her answer sounded more like a question than a statement.

John chuckled, despite the fact that Sarah's response didn't surprise him. "Two," he revealed.

"Only two? Really? Then what's the big deal? Why is he so famous?"

Their travel mate, Dana Hanson, chimed in from the back seat. "He's not telling you the whole story, Sarah. Gein confessed to killing two people, but police think he might have murdered a dozen or so more."

"Yeah," John countered. "But the real reason he's so well known is because of all the bizarre, gross things he did with his corpses—most of which were stolen from nearby graveyards."

"Do I even want to know?" Sarah asked reluctantly. "Probably not," admitted John. "Let's just say he had macabre taste—in food and decor—and leave it at that." Sarah was more than happy to let the subject drop.

Hardware Store Haunting

"Here's our first stop," said John, as he pulled his car into the parking lot of Plainfield's local hardware store. "It's supposed to be haunted, but we're not going to stick around long enough to find out. I just want to take a quick look inside."

"What does Gein have to do with this place?" Sarah asked.

John answered, but his voice suddenly sounded eerie and detached, as if he were reading from an encyclopedia. "On November 15, 1957, Ed Gein stopped here to purchase anti-freeze. A day later, the store's 58-year-old owner, Bernice Worden, disappeared. Police discovered a trail of blood leading through the store and out the back door, so they suspected foul play. The evidence led them to Gein's farm, where they found the woman's mutilated body." He paused and then added, "Do you want all the gory details?"

"No, thank you," replied Sarah.

John smiled, amused by her squeamishness. "Anyway, since that time, a handful of employees and customers have seen Bernice's spirit carrying order forms around the store. Some have also claimed to hear her apparition talking about anti-freeze."

"Well, all right, then," said Dana. "Let's go inside and have ourselves a look."

Cemetery Creepers

True to his word, John kept the hardware store visit very brief, which brought his morbidly curious companions and him to their second stop: Plainfield Cemetery.

"Not only is Gein buried here," John informed his fellow explorers, "he also used to rob graves from here."

"Gross," said Sarah.

"You can say that again," added Dana.

Sarah followed the others into the graveyard. "So what exactly are we supposed to see?" she asked.

"I'm not entirely sure," John admitted with a subtle shrug. "Reports are pretty vague: strange sounds, ghostlike shapes, feelings of uneasiness, things like that."

"Well, why don't we go and take a look at Gein's headstone?" suggested Dana.

"We could, but we're in the wrong place to do it," John noted. "The headstone was stolen in June of 2000. And when the police recovered it, they decided not to put it back. They figured it'd get stolen again. So now it's on display at the museum in Wautoma."

"Bummer," Dana mumbled.

"Well, at least we can see where Gein is buried," John offered optimistically.

Sarah scanned the cemetery and was surprised at the twinge of disappointment she felt. "You know, this would be a lot scarier if it were dark out," she announced.

"Don't worry," answered John. "By the time we get to our last stop, the sun will be down."

And with that, the three travelers ventured farther into Plainfield Cemetery.

Farmhouse Fright

"Our last stop on the Ed Gein ghost tour is the former site of his farmhouse," said John. He slowed his car to a stop before a dark country lot. "This is it."

The land that surrounded them was thick with trees. There was a hint of a dirt path that led onto the property, but it was mostly overgrown by weeds and shrubs. In fact, the entire area looked abandoned and forgotten.

"Here?" asked Dana. "It sure doesn't look like much." "An arsonist burned Gein's house to the ground way back in 1958. All that's left is this empty lot. It's privately owned, so we can't do much more than look from here."

"So was his house really haunted?" Sarah wondered aloud. "You'd think it'd have to be, with all of the terrible things he did."

"Believe it or not," answered John, "Ed Gein himself started rumors that the farm harbored ghosts. He used to babysit local kids and told them as much."

"He used to baby-sit?" Sarah exclaimed. "There's a scary thought."

"And speaking of scary," offered Dana, "check that out." She pointed into the distance, toward the spot where Gein's home used to stand.

John's mouth dropped open. "That's—that's—that's impossible," he stammered. "The land is vacant. No one can be out there."

And yet, from within the trees, a spooky blue light shone toward the visitors, floating about 10 feet off the ground in a ghostly fashion.

"I think I've seen enough," whined Sarah, her voice breaking. "Let's get out of here."

"Yeah, I think you're right," replied John, tearing his eyes away from the strange illumination. He pressed his foot against the accelerator, and the car sped away.

No one dared to look back.

Hell's Playground

There were three bodies: an adult female and two young children. Their blood-soaked clothes and frozen expressions of terror illustrated the severity of the attacks.

"I've never seen anything like this," said one of the investigators, who had ventured to the southern Wisconsin town of Brodhead. "Murdered in a park, it's a real tragedy."

He couldn't have guessed that, from these vicious crimes, Hell's Playground would be born, and the years that followed would bring many more horrors as a result of these unsolved crimes . . .

"I thought you said we were alone," Dora Langeworth whispered, as her boyfriend kissed her ear.

"We are," said Jacob Isley. "Don't worry."

She pushed his lips away from her face and pointed toward a swing, which gently swayed back and forth. "Then why is that moving?"

"It's probably the wind," Jacob declared, leaning toward her once more.

She stepped backward. "What wind?"

The boy ceased his advance and straightened his posture, as if awakening from a dream. He stared at the moving swing and seemed to notice for the first time that, indeed, there was no wind. After a long, uncomprehending moment, he finally noted, "It doesn't make sense. The swing isn't slowing down."

Jacob stalked toward the mysterious phenomenon, with Dora hurrying after him.

Then, they heard children's laughter.

The sound caused the couple to stop in their tracks. Given the strange circumstances and the darkness of this night, it was the scariest noise they could've imagined.

"Who's there?" cried Dora. There was no answer. "Hello?" she called again.

Jacob reached toward her and clutched her hand in his. "What's going on?" he whispered.

A new noise replaced the frightful giggles: a low, guttural growl that came from within the nearby bushes.

Jacob heard Dora begin to cry. He squeezed her hand. "Just relax, act normal, and walk toward the car. Don't make any sudden moves, and we'll be fine."

Together, they backpedaled, never turning their eyes away from the spot where the sounds had originated.

Three minutes later, they were safely inside Jacob's vehicle, on the road away from the haunted park—away from Hell's Playground.

The Ridgeway Phantom

It was the legend of Wisconsin's most famous ghost that brought Christopher Mann to Iowa County. He had heard for years about the Ridgeway Phantom, which apparently haunted the region in the mid-1800s. And while some reports suggested that the ghost left town atop the cowcatcher of a train engine more than 100 years ago—never to return—other rumors had it that the old ghost still lingered in the woods outside Mineral Point.

The story of the devious spirit could be traced back to 1840, when the town of Ridgeway was the site of a grisly chain of events. A team of thugs gruesomely murdered a teenaged boy by tossing him into the fireplace at a local saloon. Understandably, the victim's companion, another young man, tried to escape from town. But the cold Wisconsin weather overcame him, and the 14-year-old soon died of exposure.

Due to these two deaths, the infamous phantom was born, and Christopher, who fancied himself as something of a ghost chaser, had high hopes of finding the shape-shifting specter.

Along with his colleague, Nathan Stober, Christopher spent several days exploring the 25 miles of road between Mineral Point and Blue Mounds. It was this stretch of land on which the Ridgeway Phantom had terrorized travelers more than 150 years ago.

"This spirit changes forms, right?" asked Nathan.

Christopher nodded. "It's been seen as the ghosts of an old woman, a young woman, a headless man, and even a few different animals."

"How are we going to know it when we see it?" said Nathan, his voice dripping with sarcasm.

Christopher smiled. "Don't worry. We'll know."

He remembered reading about the reputation that the phantom had gained by attacking passersby so many years ago. Some accounts also held that the specter haunted several locations within the county. From hotels and saloons to churches and private homes, the Ridgeway Phantom seemed to be everywhere.

Panic had gripped the area for nearly three decades during the 1800s. In fact, most travelers refused to enter the phantom's domain alone, in the dark or unarmed.

Before long, practical jokers got in on the act. Their deeds—perpetrated in the name of the phantom—added to the mythos and heightened the population's fears.

Christopher chuckled to himself, thinking of the gags he would've pulled, given the chance.

"What's so funny?" Nathan asked.

Suddenly, Christopher stopped laughing. "Shhh," he whispered. "Look at that." The ghost chaser pointed toward a shadowy cluster of trees adjacent to the road.

A glowing white orb hovered in the distance. "What in the world . . ." gasped Nathan.

The ball of light rocketed toward the two young men, moving almost too quickly to comprehend—like the fastball of a professional pitcher. Christopher and Nathan barely had time to react, flinching their heads in instinctive fright.

An instant later, the ball of light was gone.

Catching their breaths, the companions suddenly found themselves laughing hysterically. After days of searching, they were finally convinced: The Ridgeway Phantom remained.

The Murdered Mistress

It was a shining example of American architecture, but it was also the site of a gruesome Wisconsin crime. Emilie Martins couldn't shake the details from her mind as she explored Taliesin, Frank Lloyd Wright's old estate near Spring Green, so she decided to share them with her kid brother, Tyler.

"In 1909, Wright separated from his wife and, in scandalous fashion, moved to Europe with Martha Borthwick Cheney—the wife of a client. When he came back to the United States, he retreated from his hometown of Chicago and moved here."

Tyler shrugged. "What's the big deal about that?"

"Be patient. I'm getting to it," Emilie replied.

Tyler shrugged again. "Oh, okay."

"Ms. Cheney moved into Taliesin, too, and while her ex-husband, Edwin, kept custody of their kids, they were visiting her on August 15, 1914, the day of the murders."

"Murders?" exclaimed Tyler, his interest now piqued. "Ms. Cheney and her children were eating lunch in one of the mansion's dining rooms, when Julian Carlton, a 30-year-old servant from Barbados, snuck inside, playing the part of a dutiful house worker. He killed them with a hatchet right in the middle of their meal."

"He did? Why?" asked Tyler.

"No one really knows," said Emilie. "But, unfortunately, he wasn't done. The murderer moved to a second dining room, where six other guests were also eating lunch. Carlton poured gasoline under the door and set the room on fire. He used his hatchet to finish off anyone who tried to escape."

"That's really disgusting," noted Tyler, his face bearing a horrified expression.

"No kidding," Emilie agreed. "By the time he was done, seven of the nine people there, including Ms. Cheney and her children, were dead. Their bodies were brought to the cottage up ahead, called Tan-Y-Deri."

As the siblings approached the small home that stood on a hill beside a towering windmill, Emilie heard one of the workers complaining.

"It happened again," the short, muscular man explained to his colleague. "Last night, I closed up the cottage and locked the doors myself. But this morning, everything was wide open."

The lanky man next to him nodded. "That's nothing. Sometimes the lights turn on and off when nobody's in there. And a couple of people told me they've seen Ms. Cheney's ghost wandering around—inside and out of this house—wearing a long, white gown."

"Is that true?" Emilie interjected, stepping between the two workers.

Their wide eyes and gaping mouths revealed that they had not seen her coming.

"Oh, no," the shorter man corrected, scratching his cheek and desperately trying to avoid eye contact. "We were just telling a few tall tales."

But it was too late.

"Yeah, right," said Emilie, already convinced that Frank Lloyd Wright's Taliesin was haunted.

The Bray Road Beast

"That's one strange-looking dog," Scott Bray muttered, as he gazed onto the field of his Elkhorn dairy farm.

He stared toward the heavily built animal that lingered in the distance. It was larger than a German shepherd, with pointed ears, and it had long, shaggy, gray-and-black hair that covered its entire body.

As the peculiar animal wandered near Bray Road on that September day in 1989, it licked its lips greedily, ready to cause trouble.

"You're not getting near my cattle," the farmer yelled in challenge to the creature.

The "dog" glanced in Bray's direction. Then it casually turned and jogged off the other way. The Elkhorn man, however, was not convinced that it would leave his cattle alone. He followed its oversize footprints to a rocky outcrop, and it was there that he lost the critter's trail.

Unbeknownst to the dairy farmer, he had just become the first of many area residents to encounter a monster that would terrorize the region for years to come—a monster that came to be known as the Bray Road Beast.

Roadside Stranger

Lori Endrizzi tapped the brakes to slow her car. The rural area along Bray Road was dark, but she had still managed to spot the stranger who knelt beside the ditch.

She rounded a curve in the road and slowed even more to ensure that the man was okay. But as she peered out the passenger-side window, she gasped in fright.

"That's not a person!" Endrizzi exclaimed.

Instead, she found herself staring at a human-size beast. The creature, sitting less than 6 feet away, met her gaze with its glowing, yellow eyes. It bared its fangs, which glimmered at the end of a wolf-like snout.

Before she sped away, Endrizzi noted that the monster appeared to be holding roadkill in its hands—a late-night snack that it had been devouring!

The young woman floored the accelerator and didn't stop until she had safely reached her house. It was only later, when she saw an illustration at the local library, that Endrizzi was finally able to name the beast she had spied: a werewolf.

A Similar Encounter

Mike Etten had been out on the town long enough. It was March of 1990 (just a few months after Endrizzi's run-in with the monster), well past 2 a.m. It was time for Etten to get back to his dairy farm.

"Would you look at that?" the man said to himself, as he drove along Bray Road, not far from the Hospital Road intersection.

He had spotted a dark-haired animal sitting near the ditch. The beast was larger than a dog, and it was holding something in its front paws, eating it. As the car passed beside the creature, Etten noticed the beast's thick features and long snout.

The werewolf looked up at him and snarled.

"What kind of weird-looking bear was that?" muttered Etten under his breath, as he continued home.

More than a year later, when the other sightings were made public at the end of 1991, Etten realized that he had probably seen the Bray Road Beast.

Run for It!

Heather Bowey was wet and cold, but that didn't mean she wasn't having fun. The 11-year-old girl had been sledding with a few of her friends near Loveland Road—not far from Bray Road. And now, just before sunset on that snowy December day in 1990, she and her companions were on their way home.

"Hey, look," said one of the children. "There's a big dog walking through that cornfield."

Heather glanced toward the stream and, sure enough, saw a silvery brown animal strolling beside the frigid creek.

"Here, puppy!" one of her friends shouted.

A few others joined in. "Here, puppy, puppy, puppy!"

The creature looked at them quizzically, tipped its head sideways, and then—to the children's horror—slowly and methodically climbed onto its hind legs, standing upright as a human does.

The frightening monster took three lumbering steps toward the children, and then it dropped back onto all fours and charged.

Heather screamed, as did most of the kids who were with her. She spun on her heels and ran as hard and as fast as she could.

By the time she and the other children reached her house, the werewolf was gone.

Not surprisingly, the encounter led Heather's mother to contact animal control. While the 11-year-old described the bizarre tale—with the other children corroborating her story—the county humane officer concluded that Heather had probably seen a coyote.

Halloween Horror

It was October 31, 1991, a perfect night for a scare. But as Doris Gipson drove along Bray Road—near Hospital Road—a confrontation with a real-live monster was the last thing on her mind. Distracted by her car's radio, the teenage girl leaned forward to change the station.

Thump!

Her right front tire surged up and then down. Doris gripped the steering wheel and slammed on the brakes.

"Oh, no," she whispered, glancing behind her to see what she had hit.

The road was empty.

Fearing that she had injured someone's pet dog—or worse—she climbed out of her vehicle and peered into the cold darkness.

"Hello?" she called, if for no other reason than to break the eerie silence.

Suddenly, as if from nowhere, a muscular, hairy form leapt onto the road and dashed straight toward her.

Thud, thud, thud.

The scurrying sound of the would-be-attacker's heavy feet grew louder, and Doris retreated to her vehicle. She jumped inside, slammed the door closed behind her, and quickly locked the doors.

Clang!

The creature greedily clutched the trunk of Doris's car.

The teenage girl screamed and, pressing her foot against the gas pedal, she shifted the car into drive.

Behind her, she heard the sharp whistle of claws scratching against metal, as the beast—unable to maintain its grip—fell backward.

Later that evening, Doris returned to the scene, this time driving with a girl she had taken trick-or-treating.

"You would not believe what happened to me a few hours ago," said Doris. "I hit a bear, and it tried to maul me right here in this spot."

"No way," replied her young passenger. "Really?"

"Wait," whispered Doris, suddenly afraid to speak at full volume. "The bear's still here." She gestured up ahead, toward a large form on the side of the road.

"Let's get out of here, Doris."

"No argument from me," she said.

As Doris accelerated away from the beast for the second time that night, her passenger peeked outside the window. When they were safely away, she turned to Doris and said, "I don't think that was a bear."

Media Frenzy

The next day, Doris shared her strange encounter with a neighbor and showed the scratches on her car as proof. Word began to spread among the locals, and soon some of the other witnesses stepped forward with their own bizarre werewolf tales.

The reports led a local newspaper writer named Linda Godfrey to write an article (and eventually a book and a screenplay) about the strange sightings. Her story was first published on December 29, 1991, and it soon became a national sensation.

The saga of Elkhorn's Bray Road Beast was picked up by larger media outlets, and the witnesses became victims of practical jokes and ridicule.

Tourists began cruising up and down Bray Road, in hopes of glimpsing the lycanthrope. And, of course, werewolf-themed souvenirs and parties became commonplace in the Delavan and Elkhorn areas.

Where's the Wolf?

Eventually, the sightings and the hype died down, but the story never fully ended. In the months and years that followed, everyone from in-flight magazine writers and tabloid reporters to politicians and Hollywood producers found their way to southeastern Wisconsin. Each hoped to capitalize on the werewolf sensation.

Nowadays, fresh eyewitness accounts are rare, but they have not ceased all together. From a young girl who was trapped in a tree for hours—just out of the beast's reach—to the occasional travelers who spot the monster crossing in front of them, tales of the werewolf continue to be told. Whether these yarns are true, are the results of overactive imaginations, or are told by attention-seekers wishing to become a part of this legend is anyone's guess.

The Highway 12 Hitchhiker

Karri Daniels didn't need a map. Highway 12 would take her all the way from Hudson, southeast, skirting Madison, and eventually down to her grandmother's place in Genoa City. Still, she wished she knew exactly how far she was from the next town. After all, the gas tank was almost empty, the sun had set, and she still hadn't eaten.

She drove onward, daydreaming about eating a chicken burrito but guessing that she would not find a Chipotle in Baraboo.

Suddenly, in the beam of her headlights, she caught the glimpse of something on the side of the road. It startled Karri into alertness, and she instinctively hit the brakes.

Deer!

An instant later, she loosened her grip on the steering wheel. To her relief, the young woman saw that she was not about to clash with a creature of the forest. The shape she had seen was actually the silhouette of a hitchhiker.

Karri knew better than to stop, but she got a good look at the man as he tried to thumb a ride. The tall stranger had messy black hair, a thick beard, and he was wearing a green jacket. His expression was blank, hopeless, as if he knew the car wouldn't stop, but it was worth a try anyway. Karri passed the man and accelerated back up to the speed limit—her version of it, anyway. But, coincidentally, about a mile later, she came upon another hitchhiker.

She slowed a bit, glided a few feet into the left lane to give the man his space, and she took a peek at him.

He, too, had messy black hair and a thick beard. And a green jacket.

And a blank, hopeless expression.

"What in the world?" exclaimed Karri. "How can that be? It's the same man!"

A few minutes later, at a Baraboo gas station, the young woman shared her bizarre encounter with a chatty, middle-aged attendant.

Upon hearing the tale, the friendly woman laughed. "You just saw the Highway 12 Hitchhiker."

"Who's that?" asked Karri.

"It's not a 'who.' It's a 'what.' The Highway 12 Hitchhiker is a ghost."

Haunted Hotels

Hotel Hell

"Have you heard all the stories about this place?" Tracy Samuelson asked. She was standing before what used to be the Maribel Caves Hotel, better known as Hotel Hell, just outside the town of Maribel.

"Yes," said Candi Balster. "But none of them are true." The college students had made the half-hour's drive southeast from Green Bay to see the old lodge, which had burned to the ground in June of 1985. All that remained were the structure's skeletal rock walls.

"Some of them might be true," protested Tracy. "A lot of people believe this really was a hideout for famous mob bosses like Al Capone and John Dillinger. The spring water bottling plant next door could have been the cover for an illegal moonshine operation."

Candi shrugged. "I thought you were talking about the ghost stories. You know, like the one where the hotel burned down on the exact same date during three separate years, killing everyone inside."

Tracy chuckled. "And how about the man who went crazy and murdered every last person unlucky enough to be staying here?"

"No," interjected her friend, "the best one has to be the coven of evil witches that opened a portal to hell, allowing dozens of demons to escape."

"Good thing a white witch came along and trapped all of the baddies. They're confined to these grounds."

"We'd better keep an eye out for them," added Candi, between bursts of laughter. "Come on. Let's look around some more."

Ten minutes later, the girls had stopped laughing. Their visit to Hotel Hell "just for the fun of it" had turned into something else entirely.

"I'm telling you, I saw it," Tracy demanded. "There was a ghost standing at that window up there. It was looking right at us!"

"Please, calm down, Tracy. I never said I didn't believe you."

"No, but you think I'm crazy. Just like those stories we were talking about."

Candi sighed. "I don't—"

Eeeeeee!

A loud, terrifying scream filled the darkness. Forgetting their disagreement, the girls stepped closer together.

"What was that?" whispered Candi. "Is there someone else here?"

As if in answer to her question, the sound of footsteps enveloped the two friends.

"Eeeeeee!" Another scream. However, this one had come from Tracy. "The wall, look at the wall!"

Candi followed her friend's gaze to the section of wall nearby. It was covered with fresh blood.

The terrified girls darted straight for their car.

Suddenly, Tracy shrieked, "Get away from me. Don't touch me!"

Candi was too afraid to look behind her. She could only imagine what horrible monsters were accosting her companion. She wheeled around the car and dove into the driver's side door. To her relief, Tracy slid into the empty seat beside her.

Too out of breath to talk, they locked their doors. Candi started the car, and they fled the premises together.

Nearly 5 miles away from Hotel Hell, Tracy at last found her voice. "I was running," she blurted between gasps. "And I felt cold hands on my back. They tried to push me down, Candi."

Staring at Tracy in awestruck silence, Candi simply nodded. All of those far-fetched tales they had laughed about didn't seem so crazy anymore.

The Karsten Ghosts

Lance Severeid couldn't wait to call his friend Thomas. He clutched the telephone, dialed the number, and waited while it rang.

"What's up?" said the cool voice coming from the other end of the line.

"Thomas, you won't believe what just happened to Tami and me."

"Really, why's that?" His voice remained even, sounding almost disinterested.

Lance pressed on, barely able to contain his enthusiasm. "We just stayed at the Kewaunee Inn. It's haunted!"

"Haunted?" Thomas's tone changed slightly, and Lance detected that he had his friend's undivided attention.

"I'm getting ahead of myself. First, let me tell you about the hotel."

Tragic History

"The inn opened in 1858, but our story truly begins when William Karsten bought it in 1911. He upsized it to a 55-room hotel and managed it, quite successfully, until his son, William Jr., took over."

Thomas sighed. "I hope this is going somewhere."

Ignoring him, Lance continued. "The elder Karsten died of a heart attack on January 4, 1940, while in his favorite suite. Coincidentally, at about the same time, his beloved grandchild Billy got sick and died at the tender age of 5."

"That's a shame," said Thomas. A new father himself, he had become much more sentimental, especially where children were concerned.

"Yeah, it is," agreed Lance. "Anyway, 26 years later, a couple of new owners decided to renovate the hotel, and that's what woke up the ghosts—all three of them."

William Karsten, Sr.

"Three ghosts?" said Thomas, skeptically. "How do you know that?"

"Just wait. That part's coming up," answered Lance, wishing Thomas could see the toothy grin on his face. "As you can probably guess, the first of the spirits is William Karsten, Sr. His apparition has been spotted drinking beer in the bar, and he's been heard moving furniture around in the room where he died."

"That's a little weird," Thomas agreed.

"But it's not all. On the second floor, some people have smelled strange odors, and some have come across unusual cold spots near William's old suite."

Billy Karsten

"Anyway, that brings us to the second ghost: young Billy Karsten," Lance continued.

"I guess he and his grandpa are inseparable," Thomas noted, a touch of sarcasm in his voice.

"A lot of people have reported hearing Billy running down the hall toward William's room. But when they checked to see who was there, the hallway was empty. Plus, some kids claimed to have played with a boy on the second floor who was described to look a lot like Billy."

Agatha

"Very creepy, but it sounds harmless enough," noted Thomas. "What about the third ghost?"

The pace of Lance's voice quickened. At last, he was getting to the part of the tale that he really wanted to tell. "That's who Tami and I encountered. Her name is Agatha."

"Agatha? Who's she?"

"Her story is kind of depressing," admitted Lance. "In 1921, she was raped by a drunken neighbor, and she got pregnant. Her mom and dad raised the child, while Agatha went to work at Karsten's hotel, living alone in room 310. Sadly, adding to her life of heartbreak, she fell in love with William, Sr., who didn't love her back." Lance paused for a moment. When Thomas said nothing, he asked, "Are you still with me?"

"Yeah, I'm here."

"Good. After 12 years, Agatha moved back home to take care of her sick dad. She stayed there for the rest of her life, never returning to the inn—at least, not until after her death."

Thomas asked, "When do you and Tami come into this epic saga?"

Lance smiled. "Guess what room we stayed in."

"Agatha's," said Thomas, not needing to wonder.

"Right, room 310. And I hope you believe this because it's totally true. You can even ask Tami. But we woke up in the middle of the night, and the room was freezing cold."

"That's not so hard to believe."

Lance ignored his friend's mocking tone. "Then, from out of nowhere, this misty figure of a woman appeared, floating through the air."

Thomas snorted. "Yeah, right."

"Believe me or don't, I don't care, but it's the truth." Thomas paused for a moment but at last said, "Go on."

"Well, Tami and I got out of there as fast as we could. We ran all the way downstairs to the front desk, although we weren't sure what to tell them. We thought they'd think we were crazy. But you know what? They knew exactly what was going on. In fact, they were the ones who clued me in to all of this stuff I'm telling you. It's even on their website!"

"Hmm, I might have to check that out."

"Yeah, and they also told us that Agatha's ghost has been seen a bunch of times, sweeping the halls, cleaning mirrors, things like that. Plus, she has a reputation as a trickster. She pushes people in the back and leaves messes of food in the kitchen."

Thomas chuckled. "This sounds like the kind of place I should spend a night in."

Lance laughed before offering a little encouragement to his friend. "You totally should."

Return of the Hanged Man

It was the state's oldest inn—and perhaps its most haunted. Built in Mineral Point in the southwest corner of Wisconsin, the Walker House had an infamous past, but that wasn't going to stop Ted Landon, a local artist, from purchasing and restoring the decrepit building.

The Walker House had gained its dark reputation on November 1, 1842, the day on which William Caffee was hanged in front of 4,000 spectators. Condemned to death for shooting another man during a fight, Caffee grew into something of a legend due to the contemptuous manner in which he spent his final moments: escorted to the Walker House atop his coffin, using empty beer bottles to beat the tune of the funeral march.

More than 120 years later, in 1964, Landon was heartbroken to see the sad state in which the historic building had fallen. Having closed its doors seven years earlier, the Walker House was a ruined mess.

"I'm going to buy it, and I'm going to bring it back to its glory days," Landon declared.

However, he was not prepared for the supernatural occurrences—such as phantom footsteps and the sounds of heavy breathing—that would slow and sometimes stall his efforts.

By 1978, Landon was forced to throw in the towel, selling the Walker House to Dr. David Ruf, who placed the inn's care into the capable hands of his property manager, Walker Calvert.

The paranormal incidents not only continued under the inn's new ownership, but they became more frequent and more alarming—culminating in October of 1981.

Calvert was in the second-floor porch, cleaning after a long day of work, when a burst of light appeared before him, seemingly out of nowhere.

"What is that?" Calvert said to himself, awestruck by the peculiar phenomenon.

The glob of light hovered for a moment. Then, slowly, it began to take shape: two legs, an arm, followed by another.

A moment later, Calvert was horrified to find himself staring at the specter of a man—one who had no head!

It must be the spirit of William Caffee, thought the property manager. The ghosts of hanging victims sometimes appear without their heads.

The apparition remained long enough for Calvert to notice its wrinkled gray miner's jacket. But eventually the specter faded away, slowly, just as it had appeared.

A few days later, a waitress on staff encountered a ghost too. She was alone in the bar on the inn's second floor, and as she glanced up from her task of clearing off the tables, she gasped.

The ghostly figure of a young man in his 20s stood, staring at her!

Terrified, the woman inhaled to let out a scream— but she didn't get the chance. Before she could exhale, the strange apparition disappeared, leaving her alone in the bar again.

"It was probably Caffee's ghost, just like the property manager saw," a friend of hers later suggested. "Ghosts sometimes appear as they looked earlier in their lives."

The decades since these sightings have left the Walker House with its doors closed, once more. The building can be found just outside Mineral Point, but it is no longer open to the public.

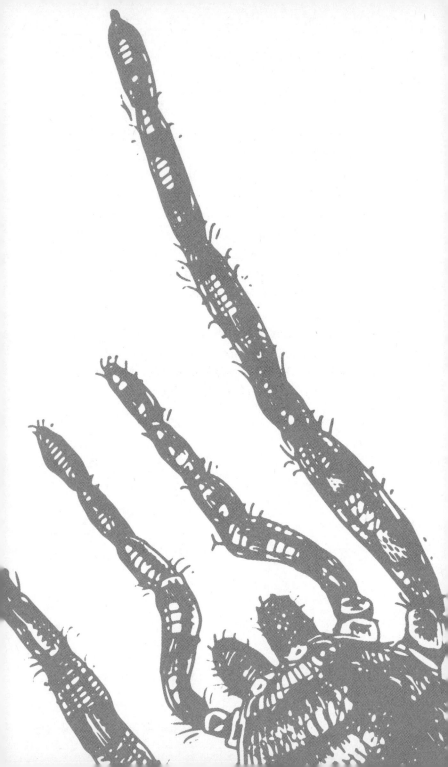

Dell House
Disturbances

Gretchen Owens knew where she was: Wisconsin Dells, a place synonymous with summer fun. And she realized that this wonderland of restaurants and roller coasters was among the state's most popular vacation destinations. But she wasn't there to "do all of the touristy stuff." She wanted to see a ghost.

She had dragged her husband, Jeremy, and a couple of their friends to the spot beside the Wisconsin River where the Dell House used to stand. Built in 1837 by a man named Allen, the old inn was a hot spot for rivermen—rugged patrons looking for food, whiskey, gambling, and women. Unfortunately, many of the Dell House's patrons probably met their maker at the bottom of the river during that violent and lawless era.

"This is the place," Gretchen announced, dropping her camping gear to the ground.

"Here?" said her husband. "Where's the Dell House?"

"It burned to the ground in 1910."

Her husband scanned the area. "Even so, shouldn't there be something left behind? A foundation? Or a stone fireplace, maybe?"

"Nope," responded Gretchen, shaking her head. "There isn't a trace of the Dell House anymore. It was entirely swallowed by the forest. Now let's get to work. We'll want to have the tents up and a fire started before dark."

The black night enveloped Gretchen, but daylight was drawing nearer. So far, no ghosts. Gretchen was beginning to believe that this trip would turn up fruitless.

Oh, well, she thought, lying awake inside the tent she shared with Jeremy. *At least we're camping.*

It was 3 a.m., and Gretchen decided to get a few hours of sleep. She was done waiting for uncooperative specters that refused to show themselves.

An eruption of riotous laughter suddenly filled the air. It sounded like a dozen drunken men standing outside, and it chilled Gretchen far more than a Wisconsin night beside a river did.

Jeremy bolted upright in bed. "What's that?"

Gretchen desperately wanted to answer, but couldn't. She thought she'd be brave. She thought she was mentally prepared for this. She wasn't. She listened in horror to the bizarre noises, and she was afraid.

To make matters worse, the joyful hysterics morphed into angry curses. Before long, the sounds of breaking glass echoed through the night, and pounding footsteps trampled around the vicinity.

As Jeremy hurriedly began dressing, Gretchen at last willed herself to speak. "Where are you going?" she said, her voice barely audible.

"Out there, to see what's going on."

"But the ghosts . . ."

Jeremy looked at Gretchen harshly, in a way that made her feel like a foolish child. "Those aren't ghosts. It's just a bunch of drunks wandering the forest."

"Way out here?" she cried.

He chose to ignore her. "I'll be right back," he said, sliding out of the tent's entrance.

Gretchen didn't wait long for Jeremy's return. Less than 2 minutes after he left, he dove back inside, practically landing on top of her. He was shaking— almost unnoticeably—and his face wore a stunned expression of disbelief.

Gretchen wrapped her arms around him. "What's wrong, Jeremy? Are you okay?"

It took him a long moment to answer, but when he did speak, his voice was empty, hollow. "You were right," he gasped. "There were people out there. They were walking around, lost. And then they were gone."

"What do you mean? They left?"

"No, I saw them. I watched as they disappeared, faded away. They were ghosts!"

The Phantom Walker

The beautiful young chambermaid couldn't help it—she was in love. Her heart almost burst with joy every time her traveling salesman returned to the Van Patten family's Evansville House (in the south-central town of Evansville), where she worked. The young woman knew that her beloved was already married, but she allowed the affair to continue for several months.

Emotions ran high, and the man soon became obsessed with his mistress. His passion turned to jealousy. He grew paranoid and became certain that his lover would leave him. And so, late one night, in the heat of the moment, the frenzied salesman strangled the chambermaid. If he could not have her, neither would anyone else.

Realizing the consequences of his actions, the man escaped from the inn and planned to catch a passing train. Once out of town, he would disappear—never having to pay for the savage crime he had committed.

However, the murdered girl was granted her retribution. Perhaps it was karma or perhaps the girl's spirit released her wrath that very night, but somehow, the salesman fell onto the tracks. Caught under the wheels of a passing car, he died a horrible death. His spirit, however, returned to the scene of his crime . . .

Mr. Van Patten sat awake in bed, listening to the heavy footfalls that paced back and forth in the hallway.

"Are you going to see who it is?" asked his wife.

He looked at her in frustrated annoyance. "We both already know. It's the same thing that's been waking us up at three in the morning every night this winter!"

"At least if you check, the noise will stop for a while," encouraged his wife.

"But no one will be out there!" he snapped.

Suddenly, the rhythm and the echo of the footsteps changed. They grew slower and more distant. Mr. Van Patten closed his eyes and crooked his head.

"It sounds like it's walking downstairs," said his wife. The footsteps continued, step after step after step.

Once they reached the first floor, those heavy-sounding boots marched toward the front door and stopped there.

Mr. Van Patten listened as the entrance was unlatched and opened, and then as the ghost continued onto the outside porch.

"Are you sure that's the ghost?" said his wife.

The owner leapt out of bed and dashed downstairs, but when he reached the front door, there wasn't a trace of evidence that anyone else had been there.

Even the freshly fallen snow outside lay undisturbed by footprints.

Despite evidence to the contrary, Mr. Van Patten became certain that the Phantom Walker had finally left for good. And, in fact, he was right. The wandering spirit was never heard from again.

Seven
Cemeteries

Bantley Graveyard

His flashlight illuminated a sign that read "Pioneers Rest Cemetery," but Eric Little knew the place by another name: Bantley Graveyard. Local legend had it that the place got its nickname because a certain Mr. Bantley killed his wife, his daughter, and himself in a nearby barn. As a result, the old cemetery was said to be haunted. Eric had come to this site, near the town of Canton in western Wisconsin, to see for himself.

"Did you hear about the boy who died here?" he asked his brown-eyed friend Tamara, who was walking rather closely behind him.

"No," she replied, a slight quiver in her voice.

Eric smiled. "Two boys were playing tag one night. One of them was running, and a mysterious hand grabbed his ankle, tripping him. The boy died of fright, instantly."

"Is that true?" Tamara asked.

The 25-year-old man stopped, causing his scared companion to bump into him. "I doubt it," he said with a low chuckle.

Through the darkness, Eric scanned the cemetery's headstones, looking for its infamous birdbath. He had been told that the birdbath was used by a demonic cult for satanic sacrifices and that, if he looked closely at it, he would still be able to see some of the bloodstains. However, the only object he found that even resembled a birdbath was a large flower planter.

"Bummer," he said at last. "I think this might have been a wasted trip." But as he turned toward Tamara, he noticed a terrified expression on her face.

Slowly, the woman lifted her arm and pointed. "Do—do—do you see that?" she stammered.

Eric followed her gaze and was instantly taken aback.

Less than 20 yards away, sitting in a tree, was the ghostly specter of a smiling little girl.

Dancing Shadows

"This place gives me the creeps," admitted Brad Zilliox. An hour north of Madison, Portage's Church Road Cemetery was perhaps the scariest-looking graveyard he had ever visited. A cluster of headstones, tucked away at the end of a dead-end road, this graveyard was—to use the cliché—in the middle of nowhere.

"No kidding," Jenny agreed. "If I were going to make a horror film, this is where I'd set it."

"Yeah, this place has a great backstory too," added Brad. "It used to be a graveyard for babies, but those headstones were removed about 200 years ago. That's why the ghost of a girl haunts the place. Supposedly, she's been spotted hanging from one of the trees."

Jenny grimaced. "If I see a little girl's ghost, I am so out of here!"

Brad nodded toward a few nearby headstones. "Would you settle for dancing shadows?"

Three black, ghostly shapes bounded gracefully from grave marker to grave marker.

Together, Brad and Jenny turned and ran.

Haunted Mausoleum

Joleen Alleckson gestured toward the large, stone mausoleum, which was flanked on both sides by headstones. "There it is," she whispered. "That's the place."

She led her best friends, twins Matt and Lisa, toward the worn, gray structure built within Green Lake's Dartford Cemetery. Situated in the limits of the eastern Wisconsin town, the graveyard was rumored to be inhabited by at least a few different spirits.

"This is where that old Indian chief is supposed to haunt, right Joleen?" said Matt, nearly tripping on a grave marker as he maneuvered through darkness.

His friend nodded. "The story is that Chief Hanageh bet another man he could swim across the Fox River. He didn't make it."

"What about the Civil War soldiers that you mentioned?" asked Lisa.

"A few of them supposedly haunt this graveyard too. If you hear any noises or get the feeling that you're being followed, it's probably them." Joleen paused, then added, "But they aren't why we're here." She stopped about 10 yards in front of the mausoleum. "Who wants to go first?"

"That depends on what we are doing," Matt answered curiously.

Joleen's eyes brightened. "It's simple, really. Just go sit on the roof for 1 minute."

"The roof of the mausoleum?" asked Matt. "That's it?"

"That's it," Joleen echoed.

Matt confidently swaggered to the mausoleum, pulled himself upward and climbed onto the arched roof. He raised his arms into the air in mock victory, and then he shrugged his shoulders. "Here I am, Jo. What's the big—"

Suddenly, Matt tumbled sideways, rolling down the roof and falling harmlessly onto the thick grass.

Lisa hurried to her brother's side. "Are you okay?" She knelt beside him. "What happened?"

The 17-year-old boy, who was 6 minutes older than his sister, looked at her, bewildered. "I was pushed," he said, biting his lower lip.

Behind them, Joleen started to laugh. Lisa and Matt turned in unison to look at her.

"You knew this was going to happen?" said Matt. "What can I say?" admitted Joleen, sheepishly. "The ghost doesn't like people on top of its tomb."

Cries in the Dark

For the five 16- and 17-year-old friends, none of the usual hangouts seemed exciting enough on that cold October night, just before Halloween. The town of Strum, which was a half-hour's drive south of Eau Claire, wasn't exactly the mecca of night life to begin with, so the teenagers decided to make their own fun.

"Let's sneak into Saint Paul's Cemetery," one of the youths suggested, and just like that the decision was made. They each had hopes of scaring the others with spooky stories and loud noises. However, none of them were ready for what they actually encountered.

The night started harmlessly enough, as the group of students roamed the graveyard well after dark. Shadows danced about, and the friends tried to convince themselves that they were seeing ghosts. But in their heart of hearts, each believed that it was just the moonlight playing tricks on them.

However, when they suddenly heard the terrifying sounds of children crying, their blood ran cold. They looked at each other in turn, from person to person, their eyes wide with a mixture of horror and bewilderment.

One of the boys said, "I think we'd better get out of here."

An instant later, the piercing shriek of a little girl rang in their ears.

All of them began to run. They raced out of the cemetery and into the safety of their car, where they promised each other that they would never again venture into Saint Paul's Cemetery at night.

Cemetery Stranger

The story was true. Of that much, Rusty Ness was sure. In the 1840s, a boy had accidentally hung himself in the hayloft of a barn near Waukesha's Tabernacle Cemetery. Now, Rusty wanted to see for himself if the old graveyard atop a hill outside town was actually haunted.

He ventured to the dark cemetery at sunset, but he was surprised to find that he wasn't alone. A short, stout man stood beside a tree, apparently deep in thought.

Rusty was disheartened, believing that the only way he would see a specter was if he were by himself.

He waited for nearly an hour. But the man wouldn't budge from his spot.

Finally, impatience got the better of Rusty. He decided to try the direct approach. He lumbered toward the stranger, who looked his way and smiled.

Suddenly, a bright flash of light filled the air, blinding Rusty for a moment. Bewildered, he rubbed his eyes and scanned the area for a possible cause. None was present.

"What in the world was—" Rusty began to say. But when he looked back toward where the man had been standing, no one was there.

Growls and Whispers

"Brandon" whispered the mysterious voice. "Who's there?" answered the nervous teen. His name was spoken again, as if by the wind.

The frightened boy turned and began walking in the other direction, toward the exit of Forest Hill Cemetery. He had entered the Wisconsin Rapids graveyard alone on a dare. It hadn't seemed too scary at the time, given that the old cemetery was located in town. But now, Brandon Schooner regretted his mistake.

As he neared the safety of Spring Street, the hushed voice that whispered his name faded away. Its sound was replaced by a second, more terrifying noise—one that caused Brandon to sprint away from Forest Hill Cemetery in a frenzied panic: the sound of growling.

The next day, Brandon returned to the graveyard with his friends. The peace and tranquility the place seemed to offer was in stark contrast to the previous night's horrors. The visitors found no evidence of the encounters that Brandon had described, but the teen remained convinced of his brush with the paranormal.

A Bloody
Waste of Time

"What a dumb idea that was," Chad Benson muttered after dropping off the last of his passengers.

He had driven three of his friends more than 45 miles from Madison, northeast to the Evangelical Church Cemetery in Juneau, with hopes of a ghostly encounter. (A lot of other people had claimed to have experienced paranormal phenomena there, including spooky figures that wandered at all hours of the night, eerily cold breezes on hot summer evenings, and even an apparition of the Virgin Mary.) Unfortunately, their trip had not been fruitful.

"It's all a bunch of lies!" Chad exclaimed, slamming his fist against the steering wheel. But, in truth, he probably wouldn't feel so upset if his friends hadn't razzed him the entire drive home.

"Wow, that was the scariest night of my life," they had said sarcastically. "When can we do it again?"

He pulled into his assigned parking spot beside the large apartment complex, locked up his beater of a car, and stormed inside. Deciding that nothing could salvage this wasted evening, he sat down in front of the television, alone within his dimly lit apartment.

Brrrring!

The telephone startled him. Chad calmed his nerves, checked the caller I.D., and decided that his friends must not be finished heckling him.

Clicking the telephone on, he said, "Hello?"

For 3 long minutes, Chad sat in silence, listening in disbelief to his friends' accounts. Then, finally, he jumped out of his chair and dashed into the bathroom—where he glimpsed his reflection in the mirror and received the jolt of his life.

Without any cause, without any explanation, traces of blood were spattered all over his hands and arms— ghostly remnants from a trip to a haunted cemetery.

Selected Bibliography

American Hauntings. www.prairieghosts.com. Troy Taylor. 2009.

Beast of Bray Road, The. Linda S. Godfrey. Prairie Oak Press, Madison, WI. 2003.

Death in a Prairie House. William R. Drennan. Terrace Books, Madison, WI. 2007.

Haunted Heartland. Beth Scott and Michael Norman. Barnes & Noble Books, New York. 1985.

Haunted Wisconsin. Michael Norman and Beth Scott. Trails Books, Black Earth, WI. 2001.

Kewaunee Inn at Hamachek Village. www.karsteninn. com. Kewaunee Inn, LLC. 2008.

Shadowlands, The. theshadowlands.net. Dave Juliano. 2008.

True Tales of La Crosse. Douglas Connell (editor). La Crosse History Works, La Crosse, WI. 1994.

Weird Wisconsin. Linda S. Godfrey, Mark Moran and Richard D. Hendricks. Sterling Publishing, New York. 2005.

Wisconsin Road Guide to Haunted Locations, The. Chad Lewis and Terry Fisk. Unexplained Research Publishing Company, Eau Claire, WI. 2004.

Wisconsinosity. personalpages.tds.net/~oldtoivo /Wisconsinosity/index.htm.

About the Author

Ryan Jacobson is an award-winning author and presenter. He has written more than 60 titles, from comic books to Choose Your Path adventures. He prides himself on writing high-interest books for children and adults alike, so he can talk picture books in kindergarten, ghost stories in high school, and other fun stuff in between. Ryan greatly enjoys sharing his knowledge of writing and book publishing at schools and special events. When he isn't working on books, Ryan likes to build LEGO sets, play board games, and try new restaurants. He lives in eastern Minnesota with his wife and two sons.